W9-BUA-485

This is the story of

Archibald Frisby

who was as crazy for science as any kid could be.

Michael Chesworth

Farrar, Straus and Giroux   New York

*To my mother the writer
and my father the scientist*

Copyright © 1994 by Michael Chesworth
All rights reserved
Published simultaneously in Canada by HarperCollins*CanadaLtd*
Color separations by Hong Kong Scanner Craft
Printed and bound in the United States of America
by Berryville Graphics
First edition, 1994

Library of Congress Cataloging-in-Publication Data
Chesworth, Michael.
Archibald Frisby / Michael Chesworth. — 1st ed.
p.   cm.
[1. Gifted children—Fiction. 2. Camps—Fiction. 3. Stories in
rhyme.] I. Title.
PZ8.3.C428Th 1994 [E]—dc20 93-35477 CIP AC

Thanks to Seven Mountains Scientific, Inc., the Pennsylvania
State University Agricultural Extension, and Cookie at
the D. M. Hunt Library, Falls Village, Connecticut, for their
assistance. Thanks also to my editor, Wes Adams.

REN'S ROOM

He liked zoology,
no doubt about that;
you could tell by the way
he looked at the cat.

He had taken apart
every kitchen appliance:
they had given their lives
in the interest of science.

Other kids his own age
he just simply ignored.
"If I played at their games,
I am sure I'd be bored."

His mom, Mrs. Frisby,
was growing concerned
because of the things
that her Archibald spurned.

One day in his room,
where he had been for hours,
she caught him red-handed
dissecting her flowers.

She was called by his school
and wondered, What next?
He'd been found at recess
with an algebra text.

Well, the good Mrs. Frisby
soon thought it horrific—
her child obsessed with
all things scientific.

So she turned off his Mac,
and she booted him out,
to a camp where he'd find
what fun was about.

He begged and he pleaded;
he let his mom know
that he had things to do
and did not want to go.

But poor Archibald—
Mom would not hear his side—
seeing force become motion,
squared himself for the ride.

When they got to the camp
she hugged him and said,
"Forget science awhile;
have a good time instead."

But old habits die hard,
and though he felt blue,
he still ran a few tests
on the Mulligan stew.

PLUTO URANUS JUPITER

NEPTUNE MARS

SATURN VENUS

While the other kids told
their tall tales by the fire,
Archibald's thoughts
were considerably higher.

When a thunderstorm boomed,
filling campers with dread,
guess who was busy
sketching clouds overhead.

On a field trip from camp,
in a cave down below,
the guide heard some things
even she didn't know.

In a contest to see
who could build the best kite,
Archibald's took first prize
with a world-record height.

The campers decided "Friz" was the man to explain to the counselors their recycling plan.

For the scavenger hunt
his group needed pine cones.
Instead, they came back
with some very old bones.

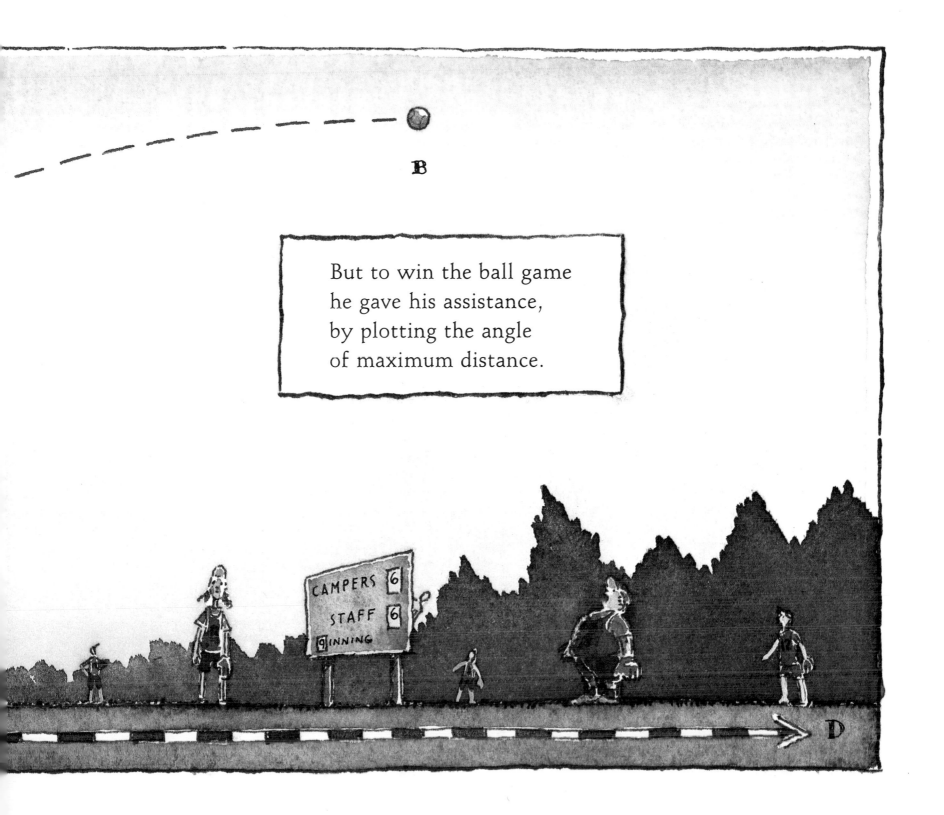

But to win the ball game
he gave his assistance,
by plotting the angle
of maximum distance.

His teammates exploded
with cheers, whoops, and cries.
It was better than winning
his first Nobel Prize.

And Archibald thought,
as he sat with his friends:
It's sad all experiments
must come to their ends.

When his mother arrived she was busting with joy. "I just cannot believe this is my little boy."

With the car loaded up
and departure time near,
Arch said, "Hey! I've forgotten
my best souvenir!"

E
C
        Chesworth, Michael
        Archibald Frisby

DEMCO